Robert
and the
Happy Endings

Also by Barbara Seuling

Oh No, It's Robert
Robert and the Great Pepperoni
Robert and the Weird & Wacky Facts
Robert and the Back-to-School Special
Robert and the Lemming Problem
Robert and the Great Escape
Robert Takes a Stand
Robert Finds a Way
Robert and the Practical Jokes

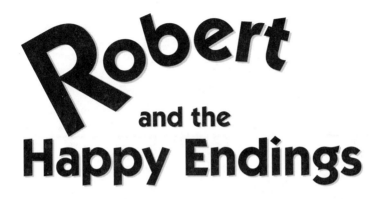

Robert
and the
Happy Endings

by Barbara Seuling
Illustrated by Paul Brewer

Cricket Books
Chicago

Grateful acknowledgment is given to the following for permission to reprint the copyrighted material listed below:
Candlewick Press, Inc., Cambridge, MA, for excerpt from *The Tale of Despereaux*. Text © 2003 by Kate DiCamillo. Illustrations © 2003 by Timothy Basil Ering. Reproduced by permission of the publisher.

Library of Congress Cataloging-in-Publication Data

Seuling, Barbara.
    Robert and the happy endings / by Barbara Seuling ; illustrated by Paul Brewer.— 1st ed.
        p. cm.
    Summary: Pirate problems plague Robert as the class rehearses a pirate play, his bike is pirated away, and bossy Susanne Lee invites only half the class to a pirate party.
    ISBN-13: 978-0-8126-2748-0
    ISBN-10: 0-8126-2748-2
    [1. Schools—Fiction. 2. Pirates—Fiction.] I. Brewer, Paul, ill. II. Title.
    PZ7.S5135Rom 2007
    [Fic]—dc22

                                                            2006100051

Contents

The New Girl 1

Pirates and Sailors 8

Gone! 15

Detective Work 22

Google™ 28

Invitations 35

Lester's Announcement 41

Rehearsing 47

Stage Fright 56

Proof 63

Surprise Party 71

Good Signs 76

Air 82

Spit 86

Faces 91

Partners 98

In-su-lation 103

The Best Packing Ever 109

Eggheads 116

In Shock 124

A Weird Plan 133

The "Bright Idea" Pin 138

Robert

and the
Happy Endings

The New Girl

Mrs. Bernthal sat on a high stool with a book open in her hands. Every afternoon, she read to the class. They were in the middle of *The Tale of Despereaux* by Kate DiCamillo.

Robert wrapped his feet around the legs of his chair and listened to Mrs. Bernthal's voice.

"*. . . no one noticed as Roscuro crawled up a table leg and onto the table, and from there flung himself onto the lowest branch of the chandelier. . . . Hanging by one paw, he* *swung back and forth, admiring the spectacle below him: the smells of the food, the sound of the music—"*

A knock on the door interrupted Mrs. Bernthal. Mr. Lipkin, the principal, opened the door and peered in. "May we come in?" he asked.

"Of course, Mr. Lipkin," said Mrs. Bernthal. "Children, what do you say?"

"Good afternoon, Mr. Lipkin," they said in unison.

"Thank you, children," said Mr. Lipkin. Next to him was a girl with blond hair, wearing a checked shirt.

"This is Taylor Jerome," Mr. Lipkin continued. "Taylor just moved into the neighborhood and is going to join your class."

Mrs. Bernthal smiled at Taylor.

Mr. Lipkin whispered something to Mrs. Bernthal. She nodded as he left.

Mrs. Bernthal looked directly at Taylor. "We're happy to have you in our class, Taylor. You will sit at Table Four," she said, taking her over to the table where Robert and Paul and Vanessa sat. "This will be your seat." Taylor sat down.

"Robert and Paul and Vanessa, will you help Taylor if she has any questions about what we're working on?" All three of them nodded.

Mrs. Bernthal continued. "Class," she said, "Taylor is hearing impaired. She is learning sign language, but she reads lips. So when you speak, be sure you are facing her."

Mrs. Bernthal picked up the book to continue their story. Robert wanted to hear what happened next, but at the same time, he was fascinated by Taylor. Could she hear anything? Could she really understand the story by reading Mrs. Bernthal's lips? Should they tell her what they were reading? He tried to get her attention, but Taylor never took her eyes off Mrs. Bernthal.

Before he knew it, the bell rang and the class was dismissed. Robert never did hear what happened in the story. He'd have to ask Paul Felcher, his best friend.

"Hey, Paul!" he shouted, running out of the school building. Paul was already outside, waiting for him.

"You want to come over?" Robert asked as they started their walk home. They almost never took the school bus on nice days, and they almost always did their homework together.

"Yeah," answered Paul. "I'll call my mom from your house."

"So what happened to that mouse that was hanging from the chandelier?" Robert asked.

"He fell into the queen's soup."

"Get out!"

"No, really!" said Paul.

"And what happened then?"

"The bell rang."

"Oh." Robert was glad he hadn't missed too much.

"We need to practice our lines," Paul said. Mrs. Bernthal had them putting on a play called *The Secret of the Pirate King*. Everyone in the class was a pirate or a sailor. Robert and Paul were Dirty Pete and Greenteeth, two of the pirate band.

"You think the new girl will be in the play?" asked Robert.

"Sure. Everyone is in it. Why?"

"She's deaf."

"But Mrs. Bernthal said she can read lips."

"So we all have to face her when we say our lines?"

"I guess," said Paul.

Robert wondered how that would work. They reached his house while he was still thinking about it.

Huckleberry met them at the door, his tail wagging.

"Hi, boy," said Robert, scratching behind the big Lab's yellow ears.

After Paul called his mom, they went upstairs to Robert's room. Huckleberry followed them and jumped up on Robert's bed. Robert and Paul dropped their backpacks there, too. Then they sat in the beanbag chair. That's where they did their best thinking. The trouble was, they were supposed to be thinking about the play, but all Robert could think about was the new girl.

Pirates and Sailors

The next day, Robert waited until Taylor looked his way before he said "Hi," and he raised his hand in a little wave, too. He wondered if that was like sign language. Taylor smiled and gave a little wave back.

It was time to rehearse their parts for the play. Mrs. Bernthal said they would have to work on their set if they were going to have the play ready in two weeks.

"Who would like to paint our set?" she asked, turning automatically to Paul. Paul

8

was the best artist in the class. He raised his hand.

"And who would like to help Paul?" Mrs. Bernthal asked. Lots of hands went up, including Robert's. "O.K.," said Mrs. Bernthal, "Lester . . . Robert . . . Lucy . . . Oh! and Taylor."

After the set painters were appointed, Mrs. Bernthal gave everyone permission to move around so they could rehearse their lines for the play together.

"Recite your lines to one another before you get up in front of the class to try them." She looked at Robert. "Robert, will you work with Taylor, please? I gave her the part of a sailor, the lookout, and she has two lines to speak. She will have to memorize them and practice them with you. Be sure she understands what she must do."

Robert looked at Taylor. She had understood, because she whirled around in her
chair to look at him.

"O.K.," he said.

Had he faced Taylor when he said that?
Did she read his lips? He said it again, just
to be sure. "O.K."

He realized immediately that it was too
loud. Kids at nearby tables stopped what
they were doing to turn and look at him.

Robert and Paul exchanged seats so
Robert could sit across from Taylor.

"You go first," he said, pointing to the pages of the script.

Taylor looked at the pages in front of her. She stared for a minute, then looked up.

"Ahoy, mates!" she shouted. "There's a ship on the horizon!"

Robert was surprised at what he heard. The last words sounded thick, like they were covered with honey and had a hard time coming out.

"That was good," he said. But Taylor's shoulders sagged.

Why didn't anyone tell him Taylor's voice would sound—different? Now they were both embarrassed. It hadn't been so bad, but no one had told him what to expect. He could have been a lot cooler about it.

"I'll do mine," Robert said, pushing his pages aside and standing up. He had memorized his lines. He had just two short

sentences to say. He pretended to have a sword in his hand. He held it high and looked straight at Taylor. "I'm Dirty Pete with the smelly feet!" he cried. "Get out of me way!"

For a moment, it was totally quiet. Then everyone at Table Four cracked up. Even Taylor. Robert was relieved. His lines had never sounded so funny before.

Later, in the cafeteria, Robert and Paul were standing in line to get their milk when Robert noticed Taylor sitting alone at a table. A few girls were at the same table, but they were talking among themselves, and Taylor was sitting apart from them.

"Look," said Robert.

Paul turned to look. "What?" he asked.

"Taylor. The new girl. She's sitting by herself."

Paul nodded. "Want to sit with her?"

"Maybe." Robert wasn't sure. What would they say? What if Taylor sounded funny again, and it showed on his face?

"O.K.," said Paul.

They got their milk and walked over to the table where Taylor sat. She looked up. The look on her face told Robert they had done the right thing.

"Hi," he said. "I'm Dirty Pete with the smelly feet. Can we sit here?"

Taylor smiled.

Paul slid in next to Robert. "Hi," he said. "Greenteeth here."

Taylor smiled. "Hi," she said. It didn't come out funny. It sounded perfectly O.K. They opened their lunches and started eating.

"What have you got?" asked Robert.

Taylor looked at her sandwich. "Peanut butter," she said. Robert heard a kind of thick sound, but he could understand her perfectly. "And an apple." She held up the apple.

"I have baloney," said Robert. He opened his sandwich and ate the baloney off the top, leaving the bread. "Oh, and chocolate-covered jelly cookies."

"Salami," said Paul, showing his sandwich. "And a brownie."

This wasn't hard at all. Robert felt himself relaxing as they ate their sandwiches and sipped their milk noisily through their straws.

Gone!

"Too bad Lester and Lucy couldn't make it this afternoon," said Paul, locking his bike to the bike rack outside the library.

"And Taylor," Robert reminded him, leaning his bike against the rack. "Don't forget she's a part of the team."

"Right," said Paul. "I'm still getting used to having a new kid in class."

"I know," said Robert. He was glad Paul said "a new kid." The other kids referred to Taylor as "the deaf girl." He didn't think that was too cool.

Robert wondered if he was the only one who thought about Taylor's deafness so much. He didn't feel like asking Paul about it right now, even though Paul was his best friend. He had to think about it more first.

They went into the library and found books about ships with good pictures. Paul's idea was to paint a backdrop of the sea, with cardboard waves moving up and down in front of it. Then he wanted to paint the pirate ship in three different sizes so he could start with the small one, looking like it was far away, and change it to the bigger ones as it got closer.

"So," said Paul, "we're looking for ships from long ago, the kind that had sails."

They went through book after book, until they finally found the pictures they needed. They checked out six books and split them up so each could carry three books in his backpack.

When they got outside, there was only one bike—Paul's—locked to the rack.

"My bike is gone!" cried Robert. "Somebody stole my bike!"

"Oh no," said Paul. "Wasn't it locked?"

Robert felt stupid. "No. I just leaned it against the rack."

Paul didn't say anything, but Robert knew he must be thinking: What a dope he is for not locking his bicycle.

They walked home slowly. It took them a long time, but that wasn't the part that hurt. Who would take his bicycle like that? In broad daylight? In front of the library?

When they got to Paul's corner, Robert didn't feel like stopping at Paul's to work on the play or do homework. He had to get home to tell his parents about his bike.

"I'll call you later," said Paul. He sounded so sad. Robert gave him a little wave to show he knew that Paul understood, and walked the last two blocks to his house. He hoped someone—one of his parents, at least—would be home. His brother, Charlie, would probably be at hockey practice.

"Robbie, is that you?" called his mom. Huckleberry was already at his feet, waiting for his usual welcoming pat. Robert was glad to hear his mom was there.

"Yeah, it's me, Mom." He dragged himself into the kitchen, where his mom was making a cup of tea. He sat down at the table and let out a sigh.

Huckleberry seemed to understand. He nuzzled Robert's hand.

"What's the matter, Rob?" asked his mom.

"Somebody stole my bike," he replied.

"What? Your bike? How? Where? When?" His mother sat down at the table with him. She seemed to be as upset as he had been.

"From in front of the library. Just now. And I don't know how, Mom."

"Was it locked?"

"Um . . . no." Robert couldn't bear to look at his mother. He knew what was coming next.

"Oh, Rob. Haven't I told you a thousand times to lock up your bicycle when you're not using it?"

He nodded. He already felt stupid. He wished he didn't have to feel even more stupid.

Robert's dad walked in from the living room. Charlie was right behind him. "Your bike was stolen?" Charlie asked.

Robert felt his neck itch.

His mom got up and reached for the phone. "I'm reporting it," she said. "If someone around here has it, the police will find it."

Robert's dad raised his eyebrows. He didn't look so sure. Robert felt himself slink down on the chair. He wished he could become invisible.

Within minutes, a police car drove up the Dorfmans' driveway. Two men in uniform came to the door.

"Come in," said Mrs. Dorfman.

At another time, this might have been interesting—even exciting—but Robert felt too sad to appreciate it.

The policemen were very nice. They both asked questions, and the taller man took down all the information in a little notebook. The shorter one said Huckleberry looked like a great dog. At the very end, though, as they were leaving, one of the policemen said they would do their best, but from past experience, it was unlikely they would recover the bike.

Detective Work

It didn't take long the next morning until every kid in the class had heard about Robert's bike being stolen.

Everyone seemed upset, even Susanne Lee Rodgers, who usually looked at Robert like he was lower than a worm.

"That's awful, Robert," she said.

Vanessa was really sympathetic. "I'm so sorry, Robert," she said. "I have a bike, and it's pink, but you can borrow it anytime."

Robert thought that was really nice. He wouldn't be caught dead riding a girl's pink bike, but he knew she was trying to help.

"Thanks," he said, making an effort to smile. He didn't feel much like smiling.

Lester Willis seemed to take it hardest of all. "I wish I had been there," he said. "Maybe it wouldn't have happened. But I had to help my dad on his route." Lester's dad was in the trash-removal business.

The other kids pitched in enthusiastically.

"We can look out for it wherever we go," said Kristi Mills.

"What does it look like?" asked Emily Asher.

Paul jumped in. "I'll draw it! Then we can each make a copy to help identify the bike."

Robert was flabbergasted at all the help the kids offered. He described the bike as Paul drew it.

He described the handlebars with the blue grips and the tassels.

He described the bell that was clamped
onto the handlebars.

He described the color—blue—and the
white racing stripe on the frame and on
the fenders.

He described the light in the front.

He described the reflectors on the pedals
and in the back.

And he described the ten-speed hand
brakes.

"Wow," said Joey Rizzo. "You really know your bike, don't you?"

"Yeah," said Robert. "I love that bike." He tried hard not to cry.

Mrs. Bernthal took the bicycle picture and offered to make photocopies in the office at lunchtime.

"Let's get to work now," she called. "Tomorrow you will say your parts in front of the class, and I hope you will have them memorized."

"When do we work on our costumes?" asked Kristi.

"I think you can start working on them anytime," said Mrs. Bernthal. "But don't neglect learning your lines to work on the costumes."

"Oh, great!" said Kristi. She and Emily had volunteered to be on the Costumes Committee.

"What about the props? When do we

25

bring those in?" asked Brian Hoberman. He and Matt Blakey were the Props Committee.

"You can bring those in, and we'll just keep them here for when we need them," said Mrs. Bernthal. "If you have any other questions about what and when, ask Susanne Lee. She's the stage manager and has the schedule of when we will need everything."

"I have a real sword I can bring in," Taylor said. Robert and Paul and Vanessa all turned to look at her. She didn't say much, so when she did speak, everyone listened.

"A real sword," said Vanessa. "How did you get a real sword?"

Taylor shrugged. "My grandfather collected military stuff. It was his."

"Thank you, Taylor," said Mrs. Bernthal.

"That's very generous of you. But I think we'll stick to less lethal fake swords."

"But that's cool," said Robert.

"Yeah," said Paul.

Vanessa nodded in agreement.

Taylor smiled. "Thanks," she said.

Robert heard that heavy sound in Taylor's voice again. Why did it happen just once in a while?

Toward the end of the afternoon, Mrs. Bernthal handed out the papers with Robert's bicycle drawn and described.

"We'll keep our eyes open," said Joey.

"Yeah, like true detectives," said Matt.

Robert felt a little bit better knowing the kids were so willing to help him find his bike, but he couldn't forget what that policeman had said: It was unlikely they would ever recover the bike.

Google™

"**C**an I look something up on the computer?" Robert asked. He and Paul were doing their homework in Paul's room.

"Sure," said Paul. "What are you looking for?"

"You'll think I'm weird," Robert said.

"But you are weird," said Paul.

"Seriously," said Robert. "I need to find out something, and I don't want you to laugh."

"O.K., I won't laugh." Paul covered his mouth to keep from laughing.

"You're not being serious," said Robert, beginning to laugh himself.

"Well, tell me then, since I'm already laughing."

"I want to find out something about deafness."

After they got the laughing out of their systems, they settled down again. Paul went over to the computer and clicked on to the search screen.

"O.K., just type in your question," he said, getting up to give Robert the chair.

Robert sat down. He thought. Then he typed: CAN YOU EXPLAIN DEAFNESS TO ME?

A list of items came back. Robert didn't know where to begin. He was about to get up when Paul came over.

"What's the matter?"

"There's just too much. I don't know what to pick."

"O.K." Paul started over and typed in DEAFNESS.

A long list of items came up, but this time Robert read a couple that sounded good. He clicked on an information center. It was all about programs for the deaf and doctors who worked with deaf people.

He tried again. This one was titled "Answers to Your Questions About Deafness." It was interesting, and he learned that Thomas Edison, who invented the light bulb, was deaf. But it didn't answer his question.

What was his question? Did he even know? Yeah. He wanted to know why Taylor sounded funny sometimes.

"Did you find what you're looking for?" asked Paul after a few minutes.

"No."

"Sometimes you have to try again, using different words."

Robert knew he had to have "deaf" in there, but he really wanted to know about how deaf people speak. He typed in DEAF SPEECH.

Wow! This looked more like it. There was a lot about speech therapy, and sounds, and . . .

There it was! "Listen to this!" he shouted.

"What?" said Paul.

"Deaf people have the hardest time with *sh, ch,* and *th* sounds. Maybe that's it!"

Paul looked confused. Robert kept babbling. "I think that's it! When Taylor sounds funny, I think it's because the sounds she's trying to make are hard for her."

"Let's look at the script," said Paul. "Let's see. She's the lookout, right? She spies a ship." He flipped through the pages. "Here it is." He showed the script to Robert.

Robert read Taylor's lines. "'Ahoy, mates! There's a ship on the horizon!' Remember?"

"Yeah. So what?"

"So, the 'Ahoy, mates' part was O.K., but the next part sounded funny. That's because there was a *th* and *sh* in those lines." Robert made faces as he exaggerated those sounds.

He got up from the computer. "What do you think it's like, not being able to hear?"

"It sounds like . . . well . . . quiet," said Paul.

Robert laughed, but he said, "I'm serious. Think about it." He covered his ears.

Paul covered his ears, too.

"Can you hear me?" asked Robert.

"Yeah, a little," said Paul. "Can you hear me?"

Robert nodded. "Yeah, I could hear you, just not as good."

Robert pulled a tissue out of a box near Paul's bed and ripped it in half. He made two balls out of the torn tissue and stuffed them in his ears.

"Go ahead, talk."

Paul started. "I don't really know what to say, but I'm saying it, anyway. Blah-blah-blah."

Robert took out the earplugs. "You said 'I don't really know what to say, but I'm saying it, anyway. Blah-blah-blah.' But it sounded all muffled."

"Hmmm. I wonder if that's how Taylor hears," said Paul.

"That's what I was wondering, too," said Robert. He dropped the earplugs in the wastebasket.

Robert couldn't imagine what it must be like to hear nothing at all.

Invitations

When Robert sat in his seat at Table Four the next morning, some of the girls were in a cluster by the Reading Table, buzzing about something.

"What's up?" he asked Vanessa.

"Susanne Lee is having a birthday party."

"Oh." Parties didn't interest Robert, especially parties with girls. He took his notebook and a pencil out of his backpack.

Taylor was looking his way. Robert realized he wasn't looking directly at her when

35

he spoke, so she probably couldn't understand what he had said.

"We're talking about Susanne Lee. She's going to have a party." He made sure Taylor could read his lips.

She nodded that she understood.

Mrs. Bernthal asked the class to settle down. "We're having a spelling test today. Let's do it and get it over with," she said.

They groaned, but took out their pencils while Pamela Rose handed out paper.

Robert got the first few words right, but when Mrs. Bernthal gave them the word *afraid,* he froze. He never could remember if it was spelled with an *ai* or an *ia*. He picked the *ia*. That made him nervous about the next few words. When he handed his paper in, he wasn't at all sure how he had done.

It was almost a relief when they read their reports on rain forests. He knew he'd done a good job on that. He had spent a lot of time on a diorama, putting monkeys in trees and all. And it was the first time ever that he had read two books for one report.

At lunchtime, the girls were buzzing again. The word got around to Robert and Paul. Susanne Lee's parents had told her she could invite twelve friends to her party. It was going to be at Pirate's Cove, a neat restaurant where they handed out cardboard pirate hats and swords to kids and gave them their meals in cardboard treasure chests.

Robert felt a pang of jealousy. There were twenty kids in the class—no, twenty-one now, with Taylor. He didn't think he would be one of the kids invited, but he really liked those hats and swords.

"So who do you think is going?" Robert asked Paul.

Paul had a mouthful of sandwich, so he just shrugged. After he swallowed, he said, "I don't know. Who do you think?"

"I guess it's just girls," said Robert, trying not to think about those hats and swords.

"Yeah," said Paul, taking another bite of his sandwich.

Outside on the playground, Robert and Paul were horsing around when Brian blurted out to Kevin Kransky that he had been invited, and Kevin said he was, too. Susanne Lee had not handed out all the invitations yet. It was funny. Not everyone liked Susanne Lee, but everyone wanted to go to her party.

It was pretty clear by the time lunch period was over that the kids who hadn't received an invitation yet were feeling bad. They seemed to cluster together, except for Taylor, who was by herself.

Robert felt squirmy. He didn't know why it bothered him. Sometimes when they chose sides for teams, nobody picked him, and he didn't feel bad like he did now. For one thing, he knew he wasn't very good at sports. And he always ended up on a team—that was the rule. Nobody got left out.

He looked at Paul. Paul wasn't invited, either, but it didn't seem to bother Paul at all. Robert wished he could be that cool.

In the classroom, after lunch, they had to do pages in their math workbooks. Robert looked over at Susanne Lee. She was writing in her workbook. She probably knew all the answers. He never saw her erase anything.

He imagined a giant pencil eraser coming down and wiping Susanne Lee right out of her seat.

Lester's Announcement

Lester barreled into the classroom the next morning, ready to burst.

"I found it! I found it!" he cried.

Everyone looked at him.

"Found what?" asked Emily.

"Robert's bicycle! I found it yesterday when I made the rounds with my dad picking up trash."

The children gathered around as Lester continued. Even Mrs. Bernthal was fascinated. Robert was so stunned he didn't know what to say. Even the police weren't sure they'd find the bike.

"We stopped at this house, and I saw a bike leaning against a gate. It looked suspicious. The handlebars were backwards and the fenders were gone. But it still looked like that bike in the picture that Paul drew."

Lester caught his breath as he pulled the paper out of his pocket. The picture was all folded and wrinkled, like someone had really been using it.

"Then what?" asked Joey.

"A little kid came over while I was looking at it and asked me what my problem was. I told him my problem was that the bike was stolen. The kid looked scared when I said that. 'It's my brother's!' he shouted. 'Go get your brother,' I said. 'We'll see about that.' The kid ran away and didn't come back. I took the bike home with me in the truck."

"Lester, that is amazing," said Mrs. Bernthal. "But are you sure it's the bike you were looking for?"

"Yeah, I'm sure."

"When can I get it?" asked Robert. He felt a rush of excitement at the thought of seeing his bike again.

"Wait till I fix it up," said Lester. "You can't ride it the way it is."

"Great," said Robert. "How long will it take?"

"A few days. My mom says I have to do my schoolwork first." Lester shrugged. "And I have to learn my lines and paint the sets."

Robert hardly had a chance to be disappointed.

"We'll help you," said Lucy. "Come on. We'll go over your lines right now."

"And Taylor is helping us paint," said Robert, "so we'll get the backdrop done. Right, Paul?"

Paul nodded.

"O.K." Lester found his script and went off with Lucy to the Reading Table.

Mrs. Bernthal smiled. "You almost don't need me anymore," she said.

Meanwhile, Susanne Lee went around the room handing out the rest of her party invitations. Jesse Meiner got one, then Abby Ranko and Melissa Thurm.

Robert felt his stomach churn as Susanne Lee came over to Table Four. She handed one to Vanessa, then stopped next to Paul and put an invitation in front of him. It seemed like a long time before she put one down in front of Robert, too.

It was a relief, but Robert looked at Taylor. Even though there were four of them sitting at Table Four, Taylor looked all alone.

He wished he hadn't been given an invitation. It felt wrong. Why didn't he say something to Susanne Lee? Didn't she know she was being obnoxious, making people feel left out?

As they were painting away on the painter's cloth that afternoon, Robert looked at Taylor's work. She had painted the wood on the ship to look just like real wood.

"How did you do that?" he said. "That's really good."

There was no response. Taylor was working away with her brush.

Robert tapped her gently on the shoulder. When she looked up, he said again, "How did you do that? It's really good."

Taylor smiled and said, "Thank you," in that heavy-sounding way. Robert realized this time it was the *th* sound that caused it. She also touched her lips with her free hand, then moved her hand forward with the palm up.

That was the first time she'd used sign language with him, and he understood immediately that it meant "thank you." He gave her a thumbs-up. Hmmm. Maybe that was sign language, too.

Rehearsing

"**R**un!" shouted Mrs. Bernthal. Melissa was looking left and right. "Left! Stage left!" called Mrs. Bernthal. Melissa ran, first one way, then the other.

"Melissa, you must pick up your cue on time," said Mrs. Bernthal. "When you hear Robert—I mean Dirty Pete—shout, 'Get out of me way!' you run for your life. Quickly! And exit stage left."

Robert felt sorry for Melissa. The lefts and rights were really confusing. They were now rehearsing their play on the stage of the school auditorium. Mrs. Bernthal had taught them that stage left was the part of the stage on the actors' left as they faced the audience, but it was hard to remember that when you were up there onstage, and there were two doors, one on each side.

Even though he knew it was confusing for Melissa, Robert felt good, too, that he had done such a good job spooking her. As the dastardly pirate Dirty Pete, he had made himself as fierce as he could, with a black mustache and a patch over one eye, and he had jumped out at her as he shouted his line. That's probably what made her miss her cue.

Yeah, he was a pretty good pirate, if he did say so himself. Maybe he should think about being an actor someday.

They had spent all afternoon rehearsing the play. In only three days, they would perform it for their parents as well as other classes. Some kids still didn't know their lines. The costumes weren't all ready because Emily's mother had run out of fabric for the sailors' outfits.

There were still no pirate hats, and the sword for the pirate captain was just a wire hanger. Brian was supposed to make a wooden one covered with aluminum foil, but Brian was out with a cold, and nobody knew if he'd be back in time to bring the sword or even be in the play. Jesse Meiner had to learn Brian's lines as well as his own just in case Brian was still out sick on Friday.

Robert didn't know how they'd ever be able to do a dress rehearsal or be ready in time for Friday night's performance.

On Friday morning, Brian was back, with the sword, but there were still no hats. Taylor came in with a big grin on her face. Robert didn't remember seeing her that happy before. It couldn't be just the play.

He looked at her face. "What are you so happy about?"

Taylor pulled back her hair, and there was a bright red hearing aid wrapped around her ear. She pulled back the hair on the other side. There was one there, too.

"Cool," said Robert. "Can you really hear better now?"

Taylor nodded.

"No more signing?" Robert found he was a little disappointed. He liked sign language.

"Say something," Taylor said, and she turned away from him.

"Hello, Taylor, how are you today, and aren't your hearing aids bee-yoo-tee-ful?" said Robert.

Taylor turned around, laughing. "I am fine. And yes, they are bee-yoo-tee-ful," she said.

"That's great!" said Robert.

"I'm still learning to sign, because the hearing aids could break or get lost. Or my hearing may get worse." She didn't even look sad when she said that. It seemed like she just knew it was possible, and that was that. "I have to go for speech therapy," she continued, "to learn to make all my sounds correctly. I couldn't do it until I could hear the sounds clearly."

So that's what it was! Taylor couldn't hear sounds a hundred percent, so she couldn't say them properly.

"Hey look, everybody," Robert called. "Taylor's got neat new hearing aids."

The kids all came over to see.

"Cool," said Kevin.

"They're awesome," said Elizabeth Street.

"I love the color," said Pamela.

Taylor looked really happy.

"All right, everyone," Mrs. Bernthal said. "There's a dress rehearsal today. Don't forget."

They had been asked to stay after school for the rehearsal, so parents would be picking them up at four-thirty today. The school buses would be long gone by then. Robert's dad was going to come for him and Paul.

"And the performance is tonight at eight o'clock," said Mrs. Bernthal. "You must all be here by seven o'clock to get into your makeup and costumes."

Ms. Valentine, the art teacher, came

rushing in with a shopping bag. "Here are your pirate hats," she said. "I'm sorry they're so late, but they got wet, and the paint ran, so I had to do them all over again. I had the fifth grade help me during their art class. Otherwise I wouldn't have had them here on time."

The best hat of all was Lester's. He was playing the part of the Pirate King. The hat was black with a white skull and cross-bones painted on the front. When Lester put the hat on his head, he really looked like the king of the pirates.

They got through the dress rehearsal with only a few mistakes. One was that Lester forgot his lines.

"Lester, I thought you had your lines memorized better than that," said Mrs. Bernthal.

"I . . . I did," Lester stammered. "I don't know what happened."

"Don't let your costume go to your head. Practice a couple more times with someone before the performance. You can't forget your lines tonight. Everyone is counting on you."

"O.K.," said Lester, quieter than usual.

At the last minute, just as they were about to go home for the day, one of the cardboard waves keeled over, and Paul had to fuss with it and use a lot of duct tape to get it to stand upright.

Riding home with his dad and Paul, Robert wished the car would just keep on going, faster and faster, to anywhere. It's not that he didn't want to do the play; he was just so excited. He didn't want this day to be over, ever. He was having much too much fun being Dirty Pete with the smelly feet.

Stage Fright

"**R**ob! Yo, Rob!"

Robert whirled around. Lester was trying to make his way through the crowd of pirates and sailors.

"Hi!" said Lester in a robust voice, when he reached Robert.

"Hi," said Robert as he glued his mustache down with spirit gum. His dad had given him the spirit gum from his collection of horror stuff that he dressed up in every Halloween. "What's up?"

"My mom is here!"

"That's great." Robert checked the mustache in a pocket mirror Mrs. Bernthal handed him.

"She never came to anything before," Lester added.

Robert stopped fussing with the mustache and looked at Lester. He didn't know what to say. His mom and dad came to everything Robert was in. Paul's parents did, too, sometimes with Paul's little brother, Nick.

"You'll be great!" said Robert. "You're a terrific Pirate King. Wait till she sees you!"

The audience grew quiet as Susanne Lee took her cue from Mrs. Bernthal. At exactly eight o'clock, she walked out on the stage while the rest of them stayed out of sight behind the curtain.

"Welcome to Clover Hill Elementary School," said Susanne Lee. "Tonight the children of Mrs. Bernthal's class will perform

The Secret of the Pirate King by Lenore Stanley. We hope you will enjoy it. Oh, and please turn off your cell phones at this time. Thank you." She said it all perfectly.

Backstage, Mrs. Bernthal was trying to keep the noise down. "Ready, children?"

They nodded. They were ready. Except for Lester. Lester looked like he was going to barf.

"Lester, are you O.K.?" asked Mrs. Bernthal.

Lester shook his head.

"What's the matter? You know your lines, don't you?"

Lester nodded, but he looked kind of green.

Mrs. Bernthal went over to him. She took his hand. "It's O.K., Lester," she said. "Anyone can have stage fright. Some of the best actors do."

Lester was listening, but he looked scared out of his mind.

Robert wished he could do something. He knew once Lester got onstage he'd be fine. But right now, he was a mess.

"Sit down, Lester. Take a deep breath," Mrs. Bernthal said, still holding Lester's hand. "A deep breath," she said. "Take deep breaths, Lester."

Robert saw the Pirate King's hat on the floor next to Lester and picked it up. He came around and put it on Lester's head.

"Look-it here, mates," said Robert to the other kids. "It's our Pirate King. Three cheers for our king." The kids sent up a cheer. Lester smiled. He stood up.

"I'm O.K.," he said, even if he still looked shaky. He took his place by the stage door.

Mrs. Bernthal looked relieved. "Thank

you, Robert. And thank you, Lester." She opened the curtain.

Two of the pirates walked out, one with a kerchief around his head and the other with a fake knife between his teeth. They carried coils of rope that they dropped near the front of the stage. Lester came out and called to the pirates in a booming voice. "Come here, you scrungy varlets!"

The play was underway.

The cardboard waves stayed upright for almost the whole performance, and when one of them finally fell down, the actors stepped over it until it was cleared away. And when one of the backdrops caught a breeze and swayed against the back wall, someone ad-libbed, "Storm at sea!" and everyone in the audience and in the play laughed and applauded.

At the end, the audience gave the cast a hearty round of applause. Paul got a

special round for his amazing set, and he, in turn, thanked his team—Lester, Robert, Taylor, and Lucy—for helping. Mrs. Bernthal thanked each of the committees, and the parents who had pitched in to help with props, costumes, sets, and chauffeuring.

"Thank you so much for coming," said Mrs. Bernthal. "There are refreshments across the hall in the lobby. The cast and crew will join you there."

People started streaming out of the auditorium and toward the refreshment tables. Robert hurried along behind them.

He watched as Lester tried to make his way, too. But parents kept stopping Lester to tell him how terrific he was. Some took his picture. By the time Lester found his mom, he was grinning from ear to ear. So was she.

Proof

"Charlie, you really missed an excellent performance last night," said Mrs. Dorfman to Robert's older brother. She placed the box from Pete's Pizza Palace on the coffee table next to the paper plates and napkins. Pizza and movies were usually on Fridays, but this week, because of Robert's play, they were moved to Saturday.

"Yeah, I know," said Charlie, grabbing the first slice. "Dirty Pete with the smelly feet." Huckleberry stood there, wagging his tail and waiting.

Robert's dad teased, too. "We were thinking that Robert might have a career as a pirate someday, if only we lived in different times."

Robert didn't mind the teasing. He was still flying high from last night. He helped himself to a slice of pizza and put one aside to cool off for Huckleberry.

"What are we watching?" asked Charlie, looking through the DVDs on the coffee table.

"Pirates of the Caribbean," cried Robert. "Please, please, please . . ."

"I think we can accommodate Dirty Pete," said his dad. "What do you think?"

"Sure," said Charlie, planting himself in his favorite place on the couch.

Robert settled on the floor with his legs crossed, Huckleberry right next to him.

Robert took the cooled pizza slice, tore it up, and put the pieces on a paper plate for Huck, who happily scarfed them down.

Robert's mom put the disk in the DVD player, and Charlie grabbed for the remote. Just as the FBI warning came on about copying the disk, the doorbell rang.

"Hey, it's the FBI," said Charlie.

Robert laughed as his mom went to the door.

"Robert," she called a moment later. "It's Lester. For you."

Robert got up, and Huckleberry trailed

after him. Lester was at the door, all right, and he had a bicycle with him.

"Yo, Rob," said Lester. "I thought you might like your bike."

"Wow. Yeah," said Robert. He stared at the bike. It looked different.

"Come in, Lester," said Robert's mom. "We're having pizza. Would you like to join us?"

"Um . . . no thanks, Mrs. D. I have to go. My dad is waiting in the truck." He pointed out to the street. "I just wanted to drop this off."

Lester looked at Robert. "It looks different because there are no fenders. The seat was too high, so I fixed that, and I turned the handlebars back to the way they were before."

"Lester, you fixed it yourself?" said Robert's mom.

"Yeah," said Lester. "I looked at some

old bikes in the junkyard, but I couldn't find the right fenders."

Robert stared at the bike.

"Robert, aren't you going to thank Lester?" his mom asked.

"Huh? Oh yeah. Thanks, Lester." He took the bike from Lester. He rolled it back and forth. It felt O.K.

"It's a great bike," said Lester. "You can ride it without fenders, but you may want to get a new reflector light for the back of your seat."

Robert didn't know what else to say except "thank you." Was it his bike, or was it swiped from someone else? He was still wondering, but he had to say something.

"This is really great." He smiled, because his mom was watching and he knew he should. "So I guess I'll see you in school Monday, right?"

"Right," said Lester. He grinned. "You're welcome. I'm glad I had that description of your bike."

"Yeah," said Robert. But half the things in that description were no longer on the bike. How could Lester be so sure?

After Lester left, Robert settled down again and got lost in the movie, but when it was over and he got up, he saw the bike leaning against the wall near the front door.

How could he find out if Lester had brought him the right bicycle?

He called Paul and told him about the bike and his doubts.

"Well, ride it," said Paul.

"What do you mean?" said Robert.

"Just get on the bike and really ride it. You'll know your own bike once you do that."

Was that true? Robert had to give it a try.

"O.K. It's too late tonight, but do you want to go over to Van Saun Park tomorrow?"

"Sure," said Paul. "I'll be at your house after lunch."

Surprise Party

As they sailed along toward Van Saun Park, Robert stood up on the pedals and shouted.

"Wheeeeeeeee!"

Paul rode right behind him.

Whooping his way down the street, Robert felt the pedals under his feet and the grips in his hands. The seat might be slightly high, but it was his seat.

It was just like Paul had promised. Once Robert got on his bike and rode it, he knew it was his.

That Lester was something. Robert was so afraid Lester had captured the wrong bike that he didn't thank him the way he should have.

"You just thought he was taking his Pirate King role too seriously," said Paul, when Robert told him what he had been thinking.

"That's it! I thought he was being a pirate, taking what he wanted for his own good."

"Maybe YOU are the one who's taking the pirate play too seriously," said Paul, laughing.

Robert laughed. He had to agree.

They stopped by the duck pond. They laid their bikes down and sat in the grass to watch the ducks.

After a few moments just staring at the ducks, Robert blurted out, "I'm not going to Susanne Lee's party."

Paul turned to him, looking surprised. "How come?"

"Well, remember how it felt all that time while we waited to be invited?"

"Yeah. It felt terrible. But I thought you wanted to go."

"I did. I wanted to be invited like everybody else. But when I looked at Taylor, I couldn't help thinking how bad she must feel. And the other kids, too, like Lester."

"You're worried about Lester?"

"Well, you know what I mean."

"Yeah," said Paul, smiling. "He was a really great Pirate King, wasn't he?"

Robert nodded. "Everybody loved him."

There was a long silence.

"We should have our own party," said Robert.

"Susanne Lee will have a fit," Paul said. "Where?"

"My house. Your house. Wait, I know! How about Van Saun Park?" Robert felt the excitement rising.

"What a cool idea!" said Paul. "Now Susanne Lee will REALLY have a fit. A double fit."

"We can ride over on our bikes," said Robert.

"We'll have to invite everyone who isn't going to Susanne Lee's party."

"Yeah. Let's go."

They picked up their bikes and pedaled off to Robert's house to get started.

First, Robert called Susanne Lee to tell her that he and Paul could not come to her party. She had a fit, just as they had predicted. And when they told her they were going to have a party of their own, Paul was right. She had a double fit.

Good Signs

Susanne Lee pranced up to Table Four on Monday. She looked right past Taylor at Robert.

"Robert, and you, too, Paul," she said, "I think you're mean. I'm sorry I invited you in the first place." She bounced back to her table.

Robert looked at Taylor. With her hearing aids, she must have heard Susanne Lee clearly. She seemed to be writing something in her notebook, but Robert noticed that her hand didn't move across the page. She looked up out of the corner of her eye and smiled at him.

On Sunday, Robert and Paul had worked on the Van Saun Park party. Robert wrote out the invitations, and Paul did the artwork.

They gave the invitations to all the kids not going to Susanne Lee's party:

COME TO A GREAT PARTY

AT VAN SAUN PARK

NEXT SATURDAY

12 O'CLOCK NOON

P.S. EVERYONE IS WELCOME!

At the bottom was a picture of kids playing. Some of them were on bikes. An arrow pointed to one of the boys on a bike. ROBERT, it said by the arrow. Another arrow pointed to the bike. ROBERT'S BIKE, it read.

The best part was that the Van Saun Park kids now had something to talk about when the other kids buzzed about Susanne Lee's party.

Saturday was a sunny day. Robert was so excited, he got up early and took Huckleberry out in the yard to play fetch.

Huck raced after the ball, his ears flapping in the breeze. He brought the ball back and dropped it at Robert's feet.

"Good boy!" Robert hugged Huck around the neck. The dog's eyes sparkled as Robert talked to him. "Dogs are not allowed in the park," he said, "or I'd take you to the party with me." Huck licked his face as though he understood, and Robert threw the ball again.

They stayed outside for nearly an hour, until Robert's mom announced that the waffles were ready. He hoped they were the frozen kind you popped in the toaster.

They were, and Robert watched Charlie wolf down two waffles before he was finished with one. Nobody could eat as fast as Charlie.

"Robbie, I have some plastic plates and forks for your party," his mom said. "They were left over from your dad's birthday last month."

"Thanks, Mom," said Robert, stabbing his fork into a piece of waffle. "That's great."

He was glad his mom found the plastic stuff, or she might have tried baking a cake for the party. She probably would have burned it or something.

At last it was time. Paul came over on his bike, and they rode together to Van Saun Park.

"My mom's coming over in a little while with a tray of brownies," he said.

"Wow," was all Robert could say. He loved Mrs. Felcher's brownies. Other parents had said they would bring sandwiches and lemonade. This was going to be a great party.

All the kids who weren't invited to Susanne Lee's party came to Van Saun Park. Some who lived close by, like Robert and Paul, rode their bikes over. The rest came with their parents in cars. The moms spread out the food on a picnic table.

"My mom sent this," Lester said proudly. He dropped a bag of Hershey's Kisses on the table.

"Thank you, Lester," said Paul's mom. "That was very nice of her."

Lester smiled. "Yeah," he said.

"It's a feast," said Lucy. "Wow!"

"Yeah, it is," said Robert. He had not expected so much food.

"The only thing that's missing is a birthday," said Paul.

"Well, we could sing 'Happy Birthday,' anyway," said Robert. "It must be *somebody's* birthday."

They broke out singing "Happy Birthday," and when it came time to say a name, they sang "to *somebody*," and everyone cracked up, even the parents.

After they ate all they could, they went off to play while the parents clustered around and talked.

Taylor's dad set up races for them and afterward treated them all to ice cream from the snack wagon in the park.

It couldn't have been a nicer party. Not even at Pirate's Cove. Everyone said so.

Air

Back in school on Monday, the kids were all buzzing about both parties, the one at Pirate's Cove and the one in Van Saun Park.

When Susanne Lee passed Robert at the pencil sharpener, she said, "You ruined my party!"

"I did not!" said Robert, checking his pencil point. "I only invited people you didn't."

Susanne Lee looked like she would explode. Her face got very red. "I could

82

only invite twelve people," she cried. "What was I supposed to do?"

"I don't know," said Robert. "But you didn't have to make other people feel bad." He turned to see Taylor smiling at him.

Susanne Lee had nothing to say to that. She turned quickly and walked away.

Robert went back to his seat, and Paul raised his hand for a high-five.

Mrs. Bernthal tapped on her desk with a ruler. She walked over to the chalkboard and wrote in big letters: AIR.

"We are going to spend the next couple of weeks learning about air," she said. When Mrs. Bernthal introduced a new unit, it was usually exciting, but Robert wasn't sure air would be as exciting as pirates.

"You will need a blown egg," Mrs. Bernthal continued, "so please bring one to class as a part of your homework."

Elizabeth raised her hand.

"What's a blown egg?" she asked when Mrs. Bernthal called on her.

"It's an egg without its insides," said Mrs. Bernthal. "You make a pinhole at each end of the egg, then blow through one end and the egg comes out the other. The egg gets blown out without ruining the shell. Ask your parents to help you."

Robert hoped his mom had eggs in the

refrigerator. You could never tell with her. Sometimes she got busy and didn't get around to or forgot the grocery shopping. He'd check when he got home.

"Oh. One more thing," Mrs. Bernthal said. "Be very careful bringing your egg to school. A blown egg will smash easily. See how clever you can be so that your egg is safe."

That shouldn't be so hard. Robert figured he'd wrap his in a sock or something.

Spit

PFFFFFFFFFFFT! Huckleberry looked up at the sound. His ears went up. Robert blew as hard as he could into the hole at one end of the egg. Nothing came out the other end.

Robert took a deep breath and blew again. SSSPFFFFFFFFFFFT! His cheeks were tired and there was spit all over the egg and running down his chin, but the egg was still inside.

Charlie walked into the kitchen and stopped short. "What are you doing?" he asked. "EE-EW! That's gross. Why are you spitting all over that egg?"

"I'm not," said Robert.

"Yeah, you are," said Charlie, looking at the mess on the table. "What's going on?"

"I'm not spitting, I'm blowing," said Robert. "I'm supposed to be blowing the egg out."

"Is there a hole there for it to come out?" said Charlie.

"Yeah. Mom helped me make a pinhole. See?" He wiped off the egg and held it up to show Charlie.

"That's a pretty tiny hole for an egg to come through. You need a bigger hole." Charlie moved toward the refrigerator, opened it, and helped himself to a juice drink.

Robert's mom walked in. "So how are you doing with that egg, Robbie?" she asked cheerfully. She stared at Robert. "Oh my, I guess it's not going so well."

"Mom, that hole is too small," said Charlie.

Mrs. Dorfman picked up the egg with two fingers and rinsed it under the faucet. "You're right," she said. "I'm sorry, Rob. I'll fix it." She found the pin that she had used to make the hole and poked lightly at the pinhole, making it a little bit bigger. "Here, try this." She handed the egg to Robert.

His jaws still ached from all the blowing he had done, but he tried again. Sure enough, the egg started to come out in a little yellow glop.

"Wait!" cried his mom, grabbing a small bowl from the sink drainer and whisking it over to him.

Robert blew the egg over the bowl. With a few more puffs, the egg came out.

Robert washed the eggshell at the sink,

making sure no egg or spit remained on it. He set it on the table to dry and sat down.

"What should I do with the bowl?" Robert asked his mom. His foot kicked the table leg as he turned in his chair.

"Watch out!" she cried. Charlie made a dive for it, but it was too late. The egg had rolled to the edge of the table and fallen to the floor. It was smashed. Huckleberry got up and walked over to it, sniffing. He lapped it up, slurping loudly.

"Oh, what a shame! Well, you'll just have to do it again," said his mom, handing him another egg. "When you finish, put the bowl in the fridge. I'll scramble the eggs for Huckleberry in the morning."

"Remind me not to have eggs for break-fast," said Charlie. "I prefer mine without spit."

Faces

Getting his egg to school was not easy. Wrapping it in a sock wouldn't work. If he stuffed it into his backpack, his books would crush the egg right through the sock. He couldn't put it in his pocket. How could he carry it?

Robert looked everywhere for a box. A shoebox was too big. A jewelry box was too small. Desperate, he even looked in the refrigerator. There was an egg carton with three eggs in it.

With his mom's permission, he put the

three eggs in a bowl, then put his blown egg into the carton.

Paul was waiting on his corner for Robert, as usual.

"Why are you bringing a carton of eggs to school?" asked Paul.

"It's just my egg for our project," said Robert.

As they walked, Robert told Paul about the mess he had made blowing his egg.

"Yeah," said Paul, holding up his egg inside a plastic bag. "I know what you mean. Nick got hold of the first egg I was about to blow and thought it was a ball, so he threw it."

"Oh no!" said Robert. "Really?"

"Yup. He did. And I caught it. Yuck. It was gross. I had egg dripping off me everywhere."

Robert laughed. "I guess my mess wasn't so bad, then," he said.

"What do you suppose we're going to do with our eggs?" said Paul.

"I don't know. Some kind of experiment, I bet."

"I hope we don't have to blow any more," said Paul.

"Yeah," Robert agreed. "My cheeks will burst."

That morning, Mrs. Bernthal explained how they were going to use their eggs in a science experiment.

Paul leaned over and whispered, "You were right!"

Robert nodded, pleased.

"Your egg is going to be part of an interesting experiment," said Mrs. Bernthal, "so take good care of it."

The children giggled.

"You may even decorate it in some way," she continued. "Put your name on it, make a face, whatever. Your job will be to protect your egg to the best of your ability. You want no harm to come to it."

"I thought we were studying air, not eggs," Lester called out.

"Raise your hand when you have something to say, Lester," said Mrs. Bernthal. "You will soon see how air plays a big part in your experiment."

The children, buzzing now, got busy, taking out pencils and markers.

Robert made a face on his egg. It was Huckleberry, his dog. Paul drew a man's face on his. He called it Steve the astronaut.

The idea spread quickly around the classroom. Taylor made a face on hers and added two red hearing aids, just like the ones she wore.

Lester had everyone laughing. He had made his with long eyelashes and big red lips. "It's Juliet," he said. "And I'm Romeo."

He kissed his egg with a big, loud, slurping sound. Lester was pretty funny sometimes.

Susanne Lee just sucked her teeth and said, "He's pitiful," loud enough so that Lester could hear it. Lester didn't seem to care. He was having fun.

Susanne Lee refused to make a face on her egg. She just wrote her name across it:

SUSANNE LEE. Robert thought Susanne Lee would be a lot nicer if she could just have fun once in a while.

Robert was drawing whiskers on Huckleberry's face when Mrs. Bernthal made her announcement.

Mrs. Bernthal walked to the chalkboard and pointed to the word AIR. "This experiment," she said, "is to learn how to package your egg using air to protect it. We will test your packages by dropping them from different heights. Your egg should survive the fall without breaking."

This *was* going to be interesting. Robert still didn't know how air figured into it, but he figured he'd learn pretty soon.

"You are going to work with a partner for the next few days as we do our experiment." She read from a piece of paper. "Emily and Joey, you are partners. Lucy and Kevin, Taylor and Paul, Andy and

Vanessa . . ." She went down the list. Robert couldn't believe it when he heard her say, "Robert and Susanne Lee."

He groaned and slouched down in his chair. Susanne Lee was still mad at him over the party at Van Saun Park. How would they ever be able to work together?

Partners

Robert had always liked working with a partner when that partner was Paul. Then it was fun, and they laughed a lot. He didn't think he was going to laugh a lot with Susanne Lee.

Paul leaned over. "Bummer," he said.

Robert nodded in agreement. He looked over at Susanne Lee. She was not smiling. Robert slid down in his chair.

"Sorry, Huck," he whispered to his egg.

"When you work with your partner," said Mrs. Bernthal, "you can change your seat. Try it now, and show your egg to your partner."

Robert moved to Table Three, where Susanne Lee sat.

"Hi," said Robert. "This is Huckleberry. He's a dog."

Susanne Lee snorted as though a dog were a stupid thing to draw on an egg. "It's not a dog. It's an egg," she said. Her egg lay on the table plain, with no face.

Robert felt really stupid.

He was relieved when they went back to their own seats. He tried to forget about Susanne Lee during their writing session. He had trouble with spelling, but he liked to write stories. Mrs. Bernthal told them to write about someone they knew, so he wrote about Susanne Lee as The Princess Who Wouldn't Smile. He was writing about everyone in the kingdom trying to get the princess to smile, tickling her with feathers, bringing in clowns and jugglers, and still she wouldn't smile. In the end, they found out she ate lemons for breakfast. They threw away all the lemons in the kingdom, and she finally smiled.

By the time they went to lunch, Robert had almost forgotten about the egg project. Then Mrs. Bernthal reminded them of it again before the three o'clock bell rang.

"Children," said Mrs. Bernthal, "for

homework tomorrow I'd like you to bring in materials that you can use to protect your egg if it falls or is handled roughly."

Robert tucked his books into his backpack. His egg lay on the table.

"And before you leave today," continued Mrs. Bernthal, "put your eggs away carefully. We will work with them again tomorrow."

Robert looked around. He walked around the room with his egg in his hand. He was surprised that he felt protective about it. He came to the window sill, where several plants were lined up. The amaryllis was his favorite. He had seen it bloom into a big beautiful red flower, but after the flower was gone, it was just a tall thick stem with lots of long leaves around it.

It was in a big pot with a lot of soil. He touched the soil. It was slightly damp from the last watering. His finger left a small depression in the soil. He pressed harder. He pressed until he had made a deep enough depression for his egg. He placed the egg in the soil.

"Very clever," Susanne Lee said, coming up behind him. She followed his example and put hers in the soil of the plant next to the amaryllis.

Robert couldn't believe it. Susanne Lee didn't sound mad at him anymore. She had even paid him a compliment.

In-su-la-tion

Robert searched the house for something to put his egg in that would keep it from breaking.

"Mom," he said, walking into her little upstairs office, "do you have anything I can wrap my egg in so it won't get smashed?"

Robert's mom stopped tapping away at her computer and thought. She reached into a desk drawer and pulled out an envelope. "This is padded," she said, looking in, "but I think it would squoosh an egg."

"O.K. Thanks anyway," said Robert, and went downstairs to ask his dad, who was watching TV. Charlie was sprawled on the sofa, eating popcorn. A commercial was on, so Robert felt safe interrupting.

"Dad," he said, "I have to make sure my egg doesn't break. Do you know anything I can use?"

"Ho!" said Charlie, breaking in. "Is that the egg you spit on?"

"I didn't spit on it," said Robert. He turned back to his father. "Do you, Dad?"

Robert's dad looked interested. "You're talking about insulation, right?"

"No. Maybe. I don't know. It's a science experiment about air. I have to put my egg in something to keep it from breaking. What's in-su-lation?"

"Get the dictionary."

He should have known it wouldn't be that easy to ask his dad for help. Robert went over to the bookcase and pulled out the dictionary. He brought it to the coffee table and began to look up the word.

"I-N-," he said, leafing through the pages.

"I-N-S-U-L-A-T-E," added his father.

At least his dad wasn't going to make him work at spelling the word himself. He found the word. "In-su-late," he read. "1. To set apart; de-tach from the rest; i-so-late." He looked up to see if this was right.

"Go on," his dad said.

Robert continued, sounding out the words. "2. To sep-a-rate or cover with a non-con-duct-ing ma- mat- mat-er-i-al in order to pre-vent the passage or leak-age of electri-ci-ty, heat, or sound." He took a breath, not understanding a word of what he had just read.

Robert's dad explained it. "That means," he said, "that something—like air—is used to fill the space so other things can't get in."

Why did they use all those words to say something so simple? How could anyone understand it? His dad must be a genius.

"What you need," said his dad, "is something to surround your egg to keep it from being hurt by anything that might break it."

"Like if it falls?" asked Robert.

"Yes."

"What if I put it in a box?" asked Robert.

"It could roll around in the box and hit the sides, and that could break it. But if you crumpled up newspapers and put them all around your egg, all the air that's trapped in the folds of the newspaper would protect it."

Robert considered that. It made sense. There were plenty of newspapers around the house.

"You can even use this," said Mr. Dorfman, reaching over to the bowl in

Charlie's lap and grabbing a handful of popcorn.

"Hey!" said Charlie, pulling the bowl back.

Popcorn! Robert wondered what Susanne Lee would think about that.

"But you'd need plenty of it, and you'd have to fill up a box much bigger than the egg, then put the egg deep in the center of it."

Robert didn't have that big a box or that much popcorn, with Charlie wolfing it down so fast. So even though it was a good idea, he decided the crumpled newspaper was the best idea.

The Best Packing Ever

Sure enough, the next day Mrs. Bernthal explained all about how air is used as a shock absorber.

Robert's dad had been right. He had known all about this stuff.

"You know the bicycle helmets you wear?" asked Mrs. Bernthal. "And football helmets? There is a layer of air between the part that fits on your head and the hard outer shell. The air locked between the two layers is what keeps your head from getting hurt when you fall."

"In-su-la-tion," Robert whispered out loud as he doodled in his notebook.

"Yes, Robert. Insulation." She smiled at him before turning around to write it out on the chalkboard. "That's a big word that you can all look up."

Robert glanced over at Susanne Lee. Sure enough, she was looking his way. She even had a little smile on her face. Surely, he couldn't have impressed her! He slunk down in his chair and continued to doodle.

Kids had brought in all kinds of materials to protect their eggs. Emily Asher had a shopping bag full of plastic peanuts that had come with a new DVD player. Lucy Ritts brought in the cardboard container from her mom's bath powder. It still smelled like flowers. Susanne Lee brought in a mayonnaise jar filled nearly to the top with water. Her egg floated in the space at the top. Lester brought in bubble wrap and kept popping the bubbles. With all the crinkling and squooshing and popping, Mrs. Bernthal had to tap her ruler several times to get everybody quiet.

"You all seem to have the idea. Now I want you to think like inventors. Go to work and put your egg in a protective package. Remember what I told you about how air acts as a shock absorber. Your egg will have to withstand a lot of punishment."

"You mean like falling off the table?"

"Yes, like falling off the table—and worse."

"Like getting sat on?"

"Yes, that's a good example, too."

Robert wasn't sure his egg would survive getting sat on, no matter how much crumpled newspaper he used, especially if the person who sat on it was big, like Lester.

Susanne Lee was worried, too. "We need something that's foolproof," she said with determination in her eyes.

"Take your time," said Mrs. Bernthal, "and think about it carefully. Tomorrow we're going to drop the eggs on the hard floor."

There was a gasp from the class.

"But our eggs will break!" said Melissa.

"That's just the point," said Mrs. Bernthal. "It's your job to see that they don't break. Remember that air can absorb shock. Use air to keep your egg from breaking."

Mrs. Bernthal always used grown-up language with them, but they always understood her.

"Think of air bags in cars, shoulder pads that football players wear, and the sneakers you all wear. Air is a part of all those things, acting as a shock absorber.

Work together and come up with the best package possible. I'm going to mark you as a team for this project."

Susanne Lee looked at the jar of water in front of her. "This will never work," she said miserably.

Robert had thought that was a cool way to carry an egg, too, until now, but Susanne Lee couldn't drop a jar. It would break.

"What if you put your egg and water in a plastic container instead of a glass jar?" he suggested, trying to be helpful.

Susanne Lee actually thought about it. "I can try it, but I think even plastic would break if it's dropped. Or the lid would pop off. I may have to think of something else."

"What about this?" he asked, looking at his own egg in its nest of crumpled newspaper.

"I don't know. Newspaper works for just bumps and taps. But I don't think it will work falling on the hard floor. Robert, we have some work to do."

That "we" sounded scary to Robert. How could he come up with something even Susanne Lee couldn't think of?

"Think hard, Robert." Now she was using her bossy voice. "I want ours to be the best invention ever. We've got to come up with something nobody else has thought of."

Robert swallowed hard. What could they possibly think of that nobody else had thought of before? He didn't even know how to begin.

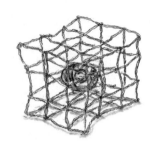

Eggheads

R obert and Paul walked to Robert's house, planning to work on their assignment together. Huckleberry met them at the door, wagging his tail so hard it looked like it would wag right off.

They dropped their backpacks beside the umbrella stand and reached down to pat Huckleberry and scratch behind the big dog's ears. Huckleberry immediately rolled over, and Robert knelt down beside him to give him a belly rub.

"Come on, Huck," he said, getting up. "Let's go play." Paul followed as they went out to the backyard for a game of fetch. Huck ran all over the yard, getting the ball and bringing it back to Robert to throw again. He never got tired of this game, unless he saw a squirrel. Then Huck would race after the squirrel, the squirrel would flee up the tree, and Huck would stand at the base of the tree barking and whining and waiting for the squirrel to come down, which it never did.

While Huck ran back and forth fetching the ball, Robert said, "Is your egg project ready?" Paul had showed Robert his idea while he was working on it. It was a cage for the egg made out of pipe cleaners.

"Not yet," said Paul. "It needs something else. I'm still working on it."

"Me too," said Robert.

"I thought yours was ready."

"I thought it was, too, but Susanne Lee thinks we need something better."

"That sounds like Susanne Lee. She has to do it better than anyone else," said Paul. "What are you going to do?"

"That's just it. I don't know. All we came up with so far is newspapers and a jar of water."

"Yeah," said Paul, scratching his head. "The jar is a problem."

"Exactly," said Robert. "I mean, eggs-actly."

Paul laughed. "I told my mom about our eggheads, and she told me *egghead* is a word used for a smart person."

"Really?" asked Robert. "You mean Mrs. Bernthal is an egghead?"

"No. It's not really a compliment," said Paul.

"Oh, I get it," said Robert. "It's someone who thinks they're smarter than anybody else, right?"

"Sort of. I guess."

Robert stopped suddenly. "Wait!" he said. "What?"

"I'm working with one. Susanne Lee is definitely an egghead!" They fell onto the grass, laughing. Huck had treed a squirrel but left his post at the base of the tree and climbed on top of them, acting like this was an even better game.

They went inside to start on their homework.

"Paul, do you want to eat with us tonight?" asked Robert's mom as they passed by the kitchen.

"Um, I don't know, Mrs. Dorfman. I have to ask my mom." He looked at Robert helplessly.

Unless dinner was takeout from the Happy Wok Chinese restaurant, chances were, dinner would be a lot better over at the Felchers' house.

"What are we having for dinner, Mom?" Robert asked, to give Paul a chance to think.

"Chinese."

Paul brightened. "O.K. I'll call my mom." He picked up the telephone, and Robert heard him say, "Thanks, Mom," as he hung up.

"I can stay," he said. He and Robert did a high-five.

"Great," said Robert's mom. "I'll call you when it's time to wash up."

They thumped up the stairs, grinning.

When Robert's mom called them for dinner, she didn't have to wait long. They were hungry. They didn't leave any shrimp lo mein or sweet and sour pork, and they would have finished the Green Jade chicken, too, if it weren't for the string beans.

Robert's mom brought out dessert—red Jell-O with fruit pieces floating in it. As Robert dug his spoon into the shimmery stuff, he stopped short.

"Mom?" he said.

"Yes, Robbie?"

"How did you get the fruit into the Jell-O?"

"Oh, that?" said his mom. "You wait until the Jell-O is almost set. Then you add the fruit. It's easy. I'll show you next time."

"Can you show me tonight?" asked Robert.

"Tonight?" she said. "You want more Jell-O tonight?"

"Not to eat. It's for a science experiment. Can you?"

"Well, sure," his mom answered. "I don't see why not."

"Great."

Robert felt a little wave of pleasure creep over him.

Paul, sitting next to him, scooped out the last of his dessert and licked his spoon. "Why do you want to make Jell-O?" he asked.

"Because Susanne Lee wants us to be the best," Robert said.

"Since when do you care what Susanne Lee wants?"

That was a good question. Usually, Susanne Lee and her bossy ways just bothered him. He hadn't forgotten how awful she had made some kids feel over those invitations to her party.

He shrugged. "I don't know. Maybe I'm turning into an egghead, too."

They both cracked up and had to be excused from the table.

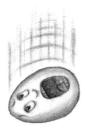

In Shock

This was Egg Drop Day. Everyone had their egghead in some kind of protective container.

Taylor had brought in a box full of plastic peanuts, and she and Paul, her partner, were putting both their ideas together. Their egg was in an elaborate pipe cleaner cage, and the cage was nestled in a bed of a gazillion plastic peanuts in a cardboard box. From the picture on the box, it looked like it had once held a coffeemaker.

Robert watched as Susanne Lee took a plastic zipper-lock bag out of her backpack. It was filled with water and had an egg in it.

"What's that?" asked Robert.

"The hard plastic containers didn't work; I tried some, and their lids popped off. I thought this might work," she answered, holding it up. "Oops!" Susanne Lee held her other hand under the bag. "It's leaking."

Robert ran to get paper towels from the supply cabinet to help sop up the water. Susanne Lee dumped her backpack out on the table. Her notebook was soaking wet. She groaned.

"I guess that didn't work," she said finally. Mrs. Bernthal handed her the pass, and Susanne Lee left the room with her leaking bag. She was probably going to the girls' room, so Robert couldn't follow her.

Susanne Lee didn't look happy when she came back. "We'll never win the Egg Drop now," she complained.

"Wait," said Robert. "I have something to show you."

Susanne Lee looked like she was only slightly interested in whatever Robert had to show her.

Robert thought of his egghead discussion with Paul yesterday. He reached into his backpack and took out a tomato sauce can with aluminum foil over the top. He opened it and showed it to Susanne Lee. She stared into the can.

"It's Jell-O," said Robert. There was Robert's egg, buried in the red stuff, looking like it was floating.

Susanne Lee's mouth dropped open.

"Robert!" she exclaimed, her eyes wide. "You're so smart. Why didn't I think of that?"

Robert had no answer. He was in shock from hearing Susanne Lee call him "smart." No one had ever called him that before.

"Do you realize what this means?" Susanne Lee squealed. Robert thought she might grab him, and he stepped back.

"Wha-what?" he stammered.

"It means we have a chance to win, you goose!" she sputtered.

"Really?" Robert wasn't used to all this excitement over something he had done.

"Well, not win, exactly," said Susanne Lee. "But our egg won't break when it's dropped. I'm practically sure of it!"

Robert smiled. "I guess," he answered. That was the point, wasn't it? He didn't see anything extraordinary about what

he'd done, but there was definitely a warm feeling inside, knowing Susanne Lee thought he was smart.

After recess, Mrs. Bernthal tapped her desk for order. The class quieted down.

"It's time for our Egg Drop," she said. Robert felt a rush.

One by one, Mrs. Bernthal called up the teams.

Emily Asher and Joey Rizzo came up with a cereal box.

"How did you protect your egg?" asked Mrs. Bernthal.

"We wrapped it in tissue paper, then packed it in a small box and then in the cereal box with crumpled newspaper," said Emily.

"O.K. Here we go." Mrs. Bernthal held the box high above her head with both hands and counted "One . . . two . . . three . . ." and let it drop.

Joey scrambled to open the box. He pulled the newspaper out. Their egg was O.K.! The children applauded.

"O.K.," said Mrs. Bernthal. "You passed the first test."

Lucy and Kevin went up next. Their egg was wrapped in a quilted baby blanket. It survived the drop, too.

Andy Liskin and Vanessa Nicolini used

a cardboard egg carton, and their egg shattered.

"Oh no!" cried Vanessa. Andy picked up the carton, and they went back to their seats.

Matt and Elizabeth had squeezed a small egg into a cardboard toilet-paper tube. It survived a bit of batting around but didn't make it through the drop.

When Robert and Susanne Lee went up, Robert held his breath as Mrs. Bernthal dropped their can. The aluminum cover fell off, but the Jell-O stayed inside and the egg was O.K.

"Yes!" shouted Robert.

Susanne Lee smiled, but Robert could tell she was thinking: Would it make it through the next test? Actually, he was thinking that, too.

"Line up," called Mrs. Bernthal, after all

the teams had dropped their eggs. "We're going to the auditorium."

Robert carried their egghead carefully. Mrs. Bernthal carried a large cardboard box. In the auditorium, she had the class watch as she placed the box on the floor in front of the stage. Then she climbed the stairs to the stage.

"You will come up front two at a time, in teams. I will drop your egg from the stage into the box. If your egg survives, you have passed the second test."

Yikes. Robert wondered if their egghead could survive such a tough test.

Team by team, the class showed its best efforts. At the end, there were seven teams left with unsmashed eggs. Robert and Susanne Lee were one of the seven teams. So were Paul and Taylor.

"Tonight you will have one more chance

to make sure your packaging is the best," said Mrs. Bernthal, "because tomorrow your egghead will be dropped from a second floor window." The children gasped. "Any team whose egghead survives this last drop will receive 'Bright Idea' pins." She held up a cool pin with a light bulb that flashed on and off. Robert wanted that pin. "So good luck to you, and may the best teams win," said Mrs. Bernthal.

Robert and Susanne Lee stared at each other. Their Jell-O egghead would never survive being dropped out of a window!

A Weird Plan

"**M**om, can we get Chinese food tonight?" Robert asked. "I need one of those takeout containers for my project."

"Well," Robert's mom said, "I was going to make a meat loaf. . . ."

"No!" Robert began, but Charlie interrupted.

"Yeah, Mom. Let's do takeout and help Robert with his project," said Charlie. Everyone preferred dinner from a restaurant to Robert's mom's cooking.

"Well, O.K.," she said.

When the order came, and they opened the containers, Robert yelled, "STOP!" before anyone could plunge a fork into the lo mein, which was mostly noodles. He grabbed the container. "Can I have this?"

"Yes, Robert, as soon as we're done. I'll wash it and give it to you. Now let's eat."

"No!" shouted Robert. Then he apologized. "I'm sorry. It's just . . . I mean . . . I want to use the whole thing."

"With the noodles?" said Charlie.

"Yes," said Robert quickly, although now he was a bit embarrassed by his outburst. He had to explain.

"Susanne Lee and I have to win when our egg is dropped out a window tomorrow. The tomato sauce can with the Jell-O isn't enough to protect it. We have to wrap it so it really can't break!"

"Since when are you such a science freak?" asked Charlie.

Robert ignored his brother. Charlie liked to tease him.

"And how are the noodles going to help?" asked his mom.

Robert continued. "We'll put the can inside the takeout container and pack noodles all around it."

"That's a weird plan," said Charlie.

"No, it's actually a good idea!" said Robert's dad. "Robert has the right concept of what absorbs shock."

Robert didn't know what "concept" meant, but it sounded like a good thing.

"You can't be serious," said Robert's mom. "He can't take lo mein to school for his project!"

"Well, lo mein is a little messy, but what about rice?" Robert's dad said. "It's not as messy, and we always have plenty left over. Besides, there's lots more air between the grains of rice than around the noodles."

Robert looked gratefully at his dad. He had never seen his dad get so excited about something he was doing for school before.

Charlie, meanwhile, reached for the sesame chicken. "I hope no one needs this for a school project," he joked.

At last, everyone was convinced that

Robert's idea might work, and after dinner they watched as he packed the rice carefully around the tomato sauce can in the takeout carton.

Robert called Susanne Lee and told her what he had done. She sounded excited. "That's great, Robert," she said. "I have something, too, and now I think we can put our two ideas together and be the best."

"What is it?" he asked.

"Meet me tomorrow morning before the bell rings, and I'll show you."

When he hung up the phone, Robert wasn't sure who he was anymore. Had he morphed into some other person? He was not used to having Susanne Lee talk to him like he actually had a brain.

The "Bright Idea" Pin

Robert ran up to Paul's corner. "C'mon," he said, panting. "I have to meet Susanne Lee before school starts."

"Why?" Paul asked, hurrying to keep up. "Why are you suddenly interested in Susanne Lee?"

"I'm not," said Robert. It was just the excitement of getting their project to work. Wasn't it?

"It's our egg package," he told Paul. "We both have these great ideas, and Susanne Lee wants to combine them for today's experiment. I can't wait to see what she came up with."

He explained about the Chinese food container and the discussion last night at the dinner table about lo mein noodles and leftover rice.

"I'm glad I didn't have to mess with that," Paul said. "I just made more pipe cleaner cages, each one bigger than the one before."

"Wow," said Robert. "That sounds cool, too." Leave it to Paul to come up with something as clever as the pipe cleaner cages for his egg. Nobody else in a gazillion years would think of anything like that. That's why Paul would probably be an astronaut someday. He was not only an artist. He was brilliant.

At the schoolyard, Susanne Lee sat on the step outside the door with her backpack at her feet.

"So where is it?" asked Robert.

"Right there," said Susanne Lee, pointing to her backpack.

"What's in there?"

"No, not in it. That's it. The backpack."

"What do you mean?" Robert pulled out the Chinese takeout container from his own backpack.

"That's cool," said Susanne Lee. "Put it inside my backpack. I've stuffed it with newspaper, so squoosh the paper down around the takeout box. Try to keep the box in the center."

Talk about brilliant! Robert had never been around so many smart people in one day. It made his neck itch!

The experiment did not take place until late morning. Robert had to struggle through spelling and math and a reading quiz before he could concentrate on the Egg Drop project again.

At last Mrs. Bernthal announced they were going to assemble in the principal's office. Mr. Lipkin was going to let them use his window for their launch pad.

"Right outside, underneath Mr. Lipkin's window, is a concrete sidewalk, so this will be a good test of your packing skills," she told them. "After each drop, you will go down into the front yard to pick up your package and bring it back up to our classroom. Once we're all back together, we'll open them."

The tension was really great now. Emily and Joey went first. Then Andy and Vanessa, and so on, until it was Robert and Susanne Lee's turn.

As soon as the backpack was dropped, they ran like the wind out the door and to the front yard to retrieve it. They each held on to a part of the backpack as they ran up to the classroom. Robert stared at

the backpack. The suspense was going to kill him.

Finally, the room filled up, and everyone was back in their project seats. Robert sat at Susanne Lee's table, the backpack there between them. It took a lot of control for Robert not to tear into it to see if their egg was O.K.

One by one, the teams opened their packages and held up their eggs to see.

Emily and Joey were the first ones to find an egg that wasn't broken. Their cereal box bubble-wrap creation had worked.

"Yay!" yelled Vanessa. Everyone applauded.

Lucy and Kevin were disappointed when their egg came out smashed. The blanket had not protected their egghead.

When it was Paul and Taylor's turn, Taylor opened the big cardboard box. Paul pulled out the newspaper. Taylor lifted out the pipe cleaner construction and handed it to Paul. One by one, Paul undid the pipe cleaners from each other. When he finally got to the last little cage around the egg, he handed it to Taylor. Taylor took the cage apart and held up the egg. It was perfect!

"Very good, Taylor and Paul," said Mrs. Bernthal, to the applause of the children. "Now, Susanne Lee and Robert."

At last!

They both reached for the backpack at once. Susanne Lee unzipped it. Robert pulled out newspaper left and right until he got to the Chinese container. Susanne Lee opened the container and turned it over on the table. Out came the tomato sauce can, along with a lot of rice. Robert took the can and lifted the foil. They looked into the Jell-O, and there was their egg, with the Huckleberry face, staring back at them, in perfect shape.

"Hurray!" someone shouted. It sounded like Lester. The class applauded.

"You have certainly worked out a clever plan," said Mrs. Bernthal.

As they went back to their seats, Susanne Lee whispered to Robert, "Thanks. This was really fun."

Robert gulped and resisted the urge to scratch his neck where it itched so badly.

"Yeah," he said. "It was."

In the end, there were five teams that won "Bright Idea" pins from Mrs. Bernthal. Robert loved his pin. Its flashing lights blinked on and off around the words I HAD A BRIGHT IDEA.

Mrs. Bernthal tapped her desk with her ruler. "And now, let's see how our story ends." She picked up *The Tale of Despereaux* and started to read. With all the excitement of the play, the bike, the party, and the egg project, Mrs. Bernthal had still

145

read a chapter of the story to the class every day. They were now up to the last chapter: "Happily Ever After."

Robert smiled as he leaned back to listen. It was just the way it should be. All good stories had happy endings.

As they walked home from school that afternoon, Robert and Paul displayed their flashing "Bright Idea" pins on their jackets.

"So now we're eggheads, too," said Paul, watching his pin flash on and off.

"Oh no!" said Robert, pretending to be dying a terrible death. "Not that!"

He and Paul cracked up.

BARBARA SEULING is a well-known author of fiction and nonfiction books for children, including *Winter Lullaby,* illustrated by Greg Newbold; *Whose House?* illustrated by Kay Chorao; and a series of books about Robert. She divides her time between New York City and Vermont.

PAUL BREWER likes to draw gross, silly situations, which is why he enjoys working on books about Robert so much. He lives in San Diego, California, with his wife and two daughters. He is the author and illustrator of *You Must Be Joking! Lots of Cool Jokes, Plus 17 1/2 Tips for Remembering, Telling, and Making Up Your Own Jokes.*